The HAPPY TIMES STORYBOOK

Library of Congress Cataloging-in-Publication Data

Krasilovsky, Phyllis.
  The happy times storybook.

    Summary: A collection of humorous stories about
familiar childhood experiences, including school,
friendship, and vacation.
    1. Children's stories, American.   [1. Humorous
stories.   2. Short stories]   I. Sanderson, Ruth, ill.
II. Title.
PZ7.K865Hap   1987   [E]   86-23373
ISBN: 0-307-15561-7
ISBN: 0-307-65561-X (lib. bdg.)

The HAPPY TIMES STORYBOOK

By Phyllis Krasilovsky

Illustrated by Ruth Sanderson

A GOLDEN BOOK • NEW YORK
Western Publishing Company, Inc., Racine, Wisconsin 53404

This book is dedicated to the girl
who arrived with the first flowers in spring,
Margaret Amanda Krasilovsky.

Contents

Foreword

This collection of stories is half fiction, half nonfiction. There really are a Margaret and Peter, though they are both grown up now. We did make a birthday calendar when Margaret was a little girl, and I did put all four of my children to sleep each night by "drawing" hilarious faces on them. Most times the prolonged good-nights ended up in tickling, giggling, etc. When I told them I was putting "Draw Us a Face" into the book, they each remembered enthusiastically the fun we had.

Two of my children are big readers, but the inspiration for the story "Peter the Bookworm" really came from a girl named Patsy, a Fresh Air Fund child who discovered the joys of reading when she was our guest years ago. She actually did bump into things because she had a book in front of her face almost all the time.

"You Are My Friend" is also mostly true because, when we traveled, my children managed to make friends with other children who couldn't speak the same language. I've always marveled at this ability in children, and I wish adults could pick it up internationally. What a better world this would be!

As for "The Christmas Tree That Grew," that was wishful thinking that may have been born subconsciously because of the Christmas tree that unfolds and gets bigger in *The Nutcracker* ballet, which I used to take my children to see at holiday time. I loved that tree so much; I suppose I decided to capture it by putting it down on paper. Wouldn't it be great if it really happened?

Phyllis Krasilovsky
Chappaqua, New York

The Christmas Tree That Grew

Margaret and Peter Adam were sister and brother. Margaret had straight hair and bangs and Peter had curly hair, but they looked alike anyway. Many people thought they were twins, except that Peter often had his nose in a book, while Margaret liked to be active.

They lived with their mother and father in a tiny apartment in a small, narrow house in the city.

There were neighbors in the building, but the people who lived there didn't know each other very well. They lived on separate floors. The Adam family lived on the first floor, which was lucky. They didn't have to climb many steps.

An old lady named Mrs. Manning lived on the second floor.

Mr. and Mrs. Martinez and their baby daughter lived on the third floor.

Every year Mr. Adam brought home a Christmas tree. The tree took up a lot of room. The Adam family had to move the furniture around so it could fit into their living room. They didn't mind. They loved having a Christmas tree.

They enjoyed decorating it. They hung red candy canes, little toys, and bright-colored balls on it. Mr. Adam strung up red, green, blue, and orange lights. The lights turned on and off like magic. It made the living room look very special.

One year, when the Adam family was planning to move to a new house in the country after Christmas, Mr. Adam brought home a live tree. Its roots were tied up in a big ball of burlap. They had to put it into a big tub and water it to keep it alive. Mr. Adam said they would plant it in their new garden.

They decorated the tree just like all the others and hid the burlap-covered roots with red material.

The tree looked beautiful, and it smelled as fresh as a pine forest. They imagined how nice it would be when it was covered with snow, and when the birds came to sit on its branches, in the garden of their new home.

Every morning, before the children went to school, they took turns watering it. It was nice having a live tree, because it made Christmas last longer!

One morning, when Margaret went to water the tree, she noticed that it seemed bigger. When she told her family, they all went to see. No, they said, she was only imagining it.

But the next morning, when Peter went to water the tree, he, too, thought it had grown. Mr. and Mrs. Adam just laughed at the idea, but Margaret agreed with Peter that it had gotten taller.

After that, the children watched the tree very carefully. Every day the tree seemed to get a little bigger. By the end of the week even Mr. and Mrs. Adam had to agree that it really was taller. The decorations and tinsel and colored balls and toys were not as close together as they had been before. Still, the family wanted to keep the tree alive, so they kept watering it.

In a few days the star at the top touched the ceiling! Mr. Adam went to see Mrs. Manning, who lived on the second floor. He told her what had happened. "Would you mind if I made a small hole in your floor, so the tree can keep growing? I could patch it up before we move."

Because Mrs. Manning lived alone, she had missed having a tree. She said she would be delighted to help.

The tree grew right through the ceiling into Mrs. Manning's apartment, and every day it got bigger. When the branches came up to her waist, Mrs. Manning took down the decorations she had saved for years on her closet shelf. She had put them away when her children moved away and her husband died.

Now she was happy to use them again. She hung up some little wooden angels and carved sleds. It made her happy to remember past Christmases with her family. She invited Margaret and Peter to come upstairs and see how it looked.

"It's beautiful!" they said. "It's just like a separate tree!"

Mrs. Manning baked them Christmas cookies, just as she had done for her own children. She gave them apple cider to drink and told them stories about her other Christmases. It was just like a party. Almost every afternoon they went upstairs to visit her, to see the tree, and to eat more cookies.

One day, when they went upstairs, they were astonished to see that the tree was touching Mrs. Manning's ceiling! She was worried, because there was no more room for it to grow.

Mr. Adam went to see Mr. and Mrs. Martinez, who lived on the third floor. He asked them if he might drill another hole to let the tree grow. "Before we move, I can fill it up again," he promised.

Mr. and Mrs. Martinez were very poor, because Mr. Martinez had lost his job as a carpenter. They had no money to buy a tree. So they were happy to say yes. In fact, Mr. Martinez helped Mr. Adam drill a nice even circle in the floor.

Mr. Adam was very impressed with how neatly Mr. Martinez worked. He asked him if he would like to build bookcases for the Adam family's new house. Mr. Martinez was glad to have some work. He went with Mr. Adam to the new house to take measurements.

Mr. and Mrs. Martinez eagerly watched the tree grow into their apartment. Mrs. Martinez made popcorn necklaces and strung them on the branches as they came through the floor. When the tree got higher, she added balls of bright-colored knitting yarn and painted nuts hung on bits of red ribbon.

When Margaret and Peter went upstairs to see it, they were thrilled. Mrs. Martinez offered them leftover popcorn and nuts. They ate them happily and played with her baby. The baby gurgled and laughed at all the attention.

Almost every day now the children went up and down the stairs to see the other parts of their tree. They enjoyed visiting Mrs. Manning and the Martinez family. They all became good friends.

Mrs. Manning invited everyone to see her part of the tree, and the Martinez family invited everyone to see theirs.

The day before Christmas it snowed very hard. The whole city turned white. The snow was so deep that no one could go outside.

Mr. and Mrs. Adam invited Mrs. Manning and the Martinez family for Christmas dinner. What a nice time they had! They were just like one big family. The lights on the tree shone brightly and made the Martinez baby laugh. They took a candy cane from a branch for her to suck on.

Mrs. Manning gave Margaret one of her own bracelets. She gave Peter a book that her son had enjoyed when he was Peter's age.

After dinner, they sang Christmas songs. Then they all went upstairs, first to Mrs. Manning's and then to the Martinez apartment, to admire the tree once again.

A few days later the Adam family moved to their country house. They took the tree down and brought it with them. Mr. Martinez patched up the two ceilings and helped to load the new bookcases he had built. He was happy because Mr. Adam had helped him find a new job in a furniture store.

Mr. Adam planted the tree in a hole he had dug in the garden. It looked very beautiful. Two red cardinals came to sit on a branch almost immediately!

One Sunday Mrs. Manning and the Martinez family came to visit the Adams in their new house. They brought presents. Mrs. Manning had made balls of suet rolled in pumpkin seeds to hang on the tree branches for the birds. Mr. Martinez had built a fine bird-feeding station and a birdhouse. "These are to thank you for sharing your Christmas tree with us," they said.

Mr. and Mrs. Adam said, "Thank YOU! You must come for Christmas dinner next year, to share the tree again. After all, it gave us new friends."

Margaret and Peter just beamed with happiness.

You Are My Friend

One winter holiday Margaret and Peter went with their parents to Mexico. When they left home, it was winter, but when they got there, it was summer. It was very warm in Mexico.

Margaret and Peter spent most of the time on the beach. They played in the sand, collected shells, or went swimming. Peter had brought his brand-new tube with him. It was shaped like a swan, and he enjoyed riding on it in the water when he wasn't reading a book.

Several times a day a procession of donkeys laden with bags of cement went down the beach. A man wearing a big sombrero hat led them along to the end of the beach, where a house was being built. When the bags and baskets were emptied, the donkeys would return for more.

One day Peter noticed a boy riding on one of the donkeys. He stared at him, thinking how lucky the boy was to have a donkey to ride.

The boy saw Peter riding on his swan tube and stared back at him, thinking how lucky Peter was to have a swan tube to ride in the water.

The donkey caravan went back and forth, so Peter and the boy saw each other several times. Peter loved the donkey that the boy rode. It had such a sweet face. Peter knew it would be fun to ride.

The boy thought Peter's swan tube was the most beautiful thing he had ever seen. Its neck was long and white, just perfect for hanging on to when a big wave came along.

The next day, after Peter had read for a while, he built a sand castle on the beach with Margaret. When the donkey caravan passed, he smiled at the boy. The boy smiled back.

"That's a nice donkey you have," Peter said, but the boy just
shrugged.

"Do you live here all the time?" Peter asked, but the boy shrugged
again.

Peter thought the boy hadn't heard him, so he asked loudly,
"What's your name?"

The boy answered, *"Habla Español?"* and this time Peter smiled
and shrugged. He remembered that Mexican people speak Spanish,
not English!

"Hup, hup!" the man in the sombrero called, and the boy and his
donkey trotted off down the beach.

19

Peter wished he could talk to the boy. He had such a nice smile, and he seemed to be about his age.

When the boy came back, he held out a beautiful shell and pointed to the castle.

Peter took it and pressed it into the wet sand so that it looked like a window.

"*Muy bueno!*" the boy said.

Peter pointed to himself and said, "Peter."

The boy thumped his chest and said, "Pedro!"

Peter pointed to himself again and said, "American."

Pedro thumped his chest and said proudly, "*Mexicano!*"

The next time the donkey passed, Pedro said, "Peter!" and gave him another shell.

"Thank you, Pedro," Peter replied.

Each time he went past, Pedro gave Peter another shell. Before long, the castle looked splendid.

"*Bonita!*" Pedro said.

Peter could tell *bonita* meant beautiful, so he agreed. "*Bonita!*" They both grinned.

On Sunday morning the donkey caravan didn't come to the beach. Peter went walking with his family and saw Pedro feeding chickens outside a small house. He called, "Hi, Pedro!"

Pedro grinned. *"Buenos dias, Señor Peter!"*

Peter said, *"Buenos dias, Señor Pedro!"* though he wasn't sure what it meant.

"That means 'Good day, Mr. Peter,'" his father said. "Pedro is the same name as Peter in Spanish."

Peter was happy to have the same name as Pedro. It was fun to try another language. When Pedro's mother came into the yard, he said *buenos dias* to her, too.

"Buenos dias," she replied. She took some bread out of an oven in the yard and offered it to Peter's family.

"Gracias," his parents said, so Peter and Margaret said *gracias*, too. They could tell that meant "thank you."

Peter liked Pedro's house. It was made of reeds and was partly open, so he could see hammocks hanging from the walls. He pointed to Pedro, to ask him which one was his.

Pedro pointed to a green hammock on the end. He closed his eyes and made snoring noises. *"Zzzzzzzz."*

Peter laughed. *"Bonita!"* he said, pretending to yawn.

Pedro bowed to invite Peter to try his hammock. Peter lay down in it, and Pedro gave it a little push. He hummed a little song, pretending he was rocking a baby. Peter closed his eyes and snored very loudly, imitating Pedro. *"Zzzzzzzz."* Then they laughed and poked each other. It was fun having a friend who couldn't talk the same language!

That afternoon, when Peter went to the beach, he was so busy building a sand tunnel that he didn't see the wind carry his swan tube into the water. Luckily Pedro did. He jumped right off his donkey's back and swam out. He reached the swan just before another wind would have carried it off. He swam back to shore and gave the swan to Peter.

"Oh, thank you, Pedro!" Peter said. He gestured to Pedro to try it out.

Pedro patted the donkey and gestured to Peter to get on the animal's back for a ride.

The next day they exchanged rides again. Peter enjoyed trotting along the water's edge on the donkey's back. Pedro loved to glide over the waves, holding on to the swan's neck.

23

When Peter's family had to leave Mexico, Peter went to the beach to look for Pedro before plane time. They greeted each other happily, but when Peter imitated a plane to show he was leaving, they both looked sad.

Pedro took a beautiful shell from his pocket and put it into Peter's hand. *"Gracias, Pedro,"* Peter said.

He took his other hand from behind his back and gave Pedro his swan tube. Pedro was overjoyed. He couldn't stop grinning. At the same time, he wasn't sure he could accept such a fine gift. He hesitated, but Peter pushed it toward him again. "Thank you, Peter," Pedro said.

Pedro got back on his donkey and trotted off down the beach. Both boys waved to each other for the last time. They smiled, and their smiles said, "I hope I will see you again, because you are my friend."

The Wonderful Birthday Calendar

One day, near the end of winter, Margaret and Peter went to a birthday party. They had a wonderful time playing games. Margaret won the prize for pinning the tail on the donkey. She wanted to play all the games again, especially pin-the-tail-on-the-donkey. She asked her mother if she could have a party for her birthday.

"Yes, I'll try," her mother said. It was hard for her to arrange things like parties, because she had a new job in an office.

"I wish my birthday would hurry up and come soon!" Margaret said.

Her father told her, "It will be here before you know it. There are only six weeks left until your birthday."

Margaret didn't know exactly what six weeks were. "Will it still be snowing?" she asked.

"I hope not!" her father said. "You arrived with the first flowers in spring. When the flowers come up again, it will be six weeks, and then it will also be your birthday."

Margaret couldn't imagine it, because it was still so cold. She pictured the weeks looking like flowers that grow very slowly from seeds.

The weeks seemed to take so long—like the time it took to put on her sweater, snow suit, scarf, mittens, and boots...or the time it took waiting for a red light to change...or the time it took waiting for a parade to come along.

So many things took a long time to come—like hot weather, so she could go swimming...or cold weather, to freeze the ice for skating...or a lot of snow to fall, so she could build a snowman.

It always took a long time until Christmas came...and until Easter came...but it took an especially long time waiting for her birthday!

"The weeks are going by too slowly," she complained. "The first flowers of spring aren't beginning to grow at all. How many times do I have to go to sleep and wake up again before my birthday comes?"

Margaret's mother said, "Let's make a calendar of the days until your birthday. Then you will know how many days are left."

"That's a good idea," Margaret said. "Let's make a calendar with windows."

The first two weeks of Margaret's birthday calendar had pictures of snow. It had pictures of a sled, a snowman, and a snow shovel in the little windows. That was because it snowed so much.

On the first warm day, when it suddenly smelled like spring was coming, Margaret drew a smiling sun that took up a whole window. She was happy to see that the sun was beginning to melt the snow.

Then Margaret got the chicken pox. She worried, because she didn't want to be sick for her BIRTHDAY....She didn't *look* like a chicken. She didn't *sound* like a chicken. But she drew a picture of a chicken on the calendar. She wrote "Peter" underneath, for Peter had the chicken pox, too.

Margaret was afraid that she and Peter wouldn't be well for her birthday. "I hope we'll get better by then," she said.

"Don't worry. You will!" her mother promised.

The next day she drew a picture of her doll with spots all over her. She said the doll had the chicken pox, too.

The next day's window had a picture of her stuffed bear with spots.

The sun shone almost every day now. The remaining snow was disappearing quickly. Margaret wanted to go outside to play. She looked out of the window longingly.

Every day now she noticed new things to put on the calendar—pussy willows budding on branches…wands of yellow forsythia stars beginning to open…ferns unwinding a little bit…a robin with a fat red breast.

She watched the robin bring its baby a worm. Then she drew a picture of it. The baby bird had no spots on it, because…neither did Margaret! Her spots had all disappeared! And so had Peter's!

Her mother said she would certainly be able to have a birthday party when her birthday came in two weeks.

Margaret was so excited thinking about the party that she drew a big circle around the date. She couldn't think of a picture, but she drew party hats, balloons, and horns in some of the other windows.

The six weeks had gone by quickly after all. They had gone by like someone gobbling ice cream very fast...like a beautiful rainbow... like a rabbit hopping...like a balloon popping...or a soap bubble disappearing.

They had gone by as fast as the candles she would blow out on her birthday cake!

Peter helped her make invitations.

They bought candy, balloons, horns, and funny hats for the party. They also bought peanuts for a peanut hunt.

They planned other games to play, like musical chairs. Then, because spring was coming, they made up a game called pin-the-stem-on-the-daisy to play instead of pin-the-tail-on-the-donkey. Their mother painted a big yellow daisy on a sheet, and Margaret helped her cut numbered stems out of green paper.

Their mother baked a birthday cake and decorated it with Margaret's name in yellow icing.

When the birthday finally came, the sun was shining and it was nice and warm, so they decided to have the party outdoors. They even had the refreshments at a table under a tree. Margaret blew out all the candles on her cake with the very first blow.

All the children had fun playing games, especially musical chairs. They played it twice! The second time Peter won the prize. It was a book, and he almost went right off by himself to read it!

The peanut hunt was exciting. Everyone tried to find where the most peanuts were hidden.

Margaret searched along the edges of the garden. She didn't find any peanuts there, but she suddenly saw some green shoots growing out of the earth. Right in the middle was a clump of yellow and white crocuses.

Her father had told her she had been born when the first flowers in spring arrived. They had bloomed right on time for her birthday!

Now Margaret knew exactly what to put in her birthday window. She drew the first flowers of spring in the circle on her wonderful birthday calendar.

Peter the Bookworm

Peter loved to read more than anything else. Everyone called him Peter the Bookworm, even Margaret. He really didn't look like a worm! That is just a name used for people who read a lot.

Peter would read whenever he could. He kept stacks of books under his bed. He read himself to sleep every night.

At breakfast time he sometimes walked into the kitchen with a book in front of his face, bumping into cabinets and chairs that he couldn't see.

Peter often read as he walked to the bus stop, so he never realized it was raining until the pages of his book got wet!

Peter always read on the school bus. He hardly every looked out the window, so sometimes he had to be reminded to get out when they got to school. The other children laughed at him. "Peter the Bookworm, we're here!" they'd say.

He didn't have time to make new friends because he even read when he ate his lunch in the school cafeteria. He usually didn't know what he was eating! He'd be so busy reading that he'd pour sugar on his potatoes and salt on his fruit salad. Sometimes he poured ketchup into his milk and buttered his bread with mustard! "Peter the Bookworm, you're making a mess!" the other children said.

On Saturdays Peter liked to go to the library to pick out books. He liked to walk between the stacks, which were like narrow canyons. He liked the colors and the designs of the book covers. He liked the way the bindings and the paper smelled. Each book was full of different, interesting facts about places he had never been to and things he didn't know about, or was full of made-up stories that were fun to read. He wished he had ten pairs of eyes so he could read ten different books at once!

Peter spent most of his allowance buying books. He liked to collect them. They were his treasures. He took good care of them, as if they were silent friends. He had wonderful collections of stories about animals, giants, monsters, elves, and insects.

Peter owned so many books that his room looked like a small library. There were bookshelves over the windows, under the windows, next to the windows, next to the doors, over the doors, against the walls, next to his fireplace, and on top of his mantelpiece.

One summer Peter, Margaret, and their parents planned to take a family camping trip. Peter did not want to go. When there was no school, he had more time to read. He couldn't see the point of leaving his precious books just to look at trees and grass, but his father said that on this trip they weren't going to do any of the usual things they did at home.

"You'll have a good time, Peter," his father said. "I'll take you fishing."

"Hurray! I love to fish!" Margaret said.

"Well, I hate to. I'd rather read," Peter grumbled.

"You'll be able to pick blueberries," Mrs. Adam said.

"Yum. I love blueberries," Margaret said.

"I'd rather read about blueberries than pick them any old day," Peter said.

"I like to read, too," Mr. Adam said, "but not all the time. You'll see that other things can be interesting, too."

It was a long journey to the mountains. Peter wished he had a book to read in the car. Instead, he and Margaret talked with their parents. Mr. and Mrs. Adam told stories about when they were children. Peter had never heard the stories before, and he found them interesting. They sang songs and had contests to see who could count the most yellow cars and who could spot the most black cows. Peter won one contest and got a prize of an extra ice-cream cone when they stopped for lunch.

As they drove along, Peter and Margaret looked out the window. They saw houses and gardens, little towns, forests, and fields. They saw hills and lakes. Everything looked beautiful and sparkled in the sunshine.

When they went through a rainstorm, everything lost its color and became all silvery and gray.

Then they saw a rainbow arching over a hillside.

The nicest things Peter saw reminded him of things he had read in his books. When he saw a cave in a mountain, he thought of the cavemen and how they had lived. The rainbow made him think of Dorothy in *The Wizard of Oz*.

After a few hours, Mr. Adam turned off the back roads onto a superhighway. That was boring. Peter wished he had something to read. He began to read the signs along the road. "Reduce speed. Curve," he read. "Thirty-five miles per hour zone. Food, lodgings, and gas bear right." The signs certainly weren't interesting.

He leaned over his father's shoulder and read all the words on the dashboard. "Fuel. Heat. Lighter." The dashboard was even more boring.

He read all the small print on a gum wrapper he found in his pocket. "45% sugar, 10% glucose, 25% gum," it said.

Since there was nothing else to read, he made up a story in his head. It was about black cows that chewed gum and drove yellow cars at thirty-five miles per hour over rainbow roads into caves that had food, lodgings, and gas.

Just when he was about to think of other ideas, the car stopped. They had arrived at the campground. It was almost dark, and they had to light a lantern so they could pitch their tent.

Mr. Adam made a fire, and they roasted potatoes. Mrs. Adam fried hamburgers and made cocoa. It was very quiet except for the noise of the crackling fire. Stars filled the sky. Peter was excited to recognize the Big Dipper from a picture in one of his books.

It was very cold, and they were tired, so they crawled into their sleeping bags. Peter was so used to reading before he fell asleep that he lay awake for a long time. Then he began to make up another story in his head, just as he had in the car. He finally fell asleep.

The next morning, when Peter crawled out of the tent, he saw that it overlooked a beautiful lake. After breakfast, the family took a rowboat out on the water. There were trees and mountains all around. Mr. Adam taught Peter and Margaret how to use the oars. They thought rowing was fun.

In the afternoon they went hiking and found some unusual rocks. Peter decided to start a collection, so every day he hiked a little farther to search for more. Once, when he was walking at the edge of the woods, he saw a beautiful deer and a fawn. He imagined they were Bambi and his mother.

They often swam in the lake. Mr. Adam taught Margaret and Peter how to do handstands in the water.

The fresh air made them hungrier, and the food they cooked outdoors tasted better somehow. They gathered wood for their campfires and fetched water from a nearby spring.

Sometimes they saw beautiful sunsets, and each night the sky looked different. Once there was a full moon that turned red, and once they spotted two shooting stars.

Since he had no books to read, Peter made up stories to himself each night when he crawled into his sleeping bag. He tried to remember them so he could write them down when he got home.

The day before they went home, Peter swam all the way to a small island in the middle of the lake. He imagined he was Robinson Crusoe, who had just landed there.

When Peter went back to school, he did not forget the wonderful time he had. He began to write stories about it so he would remember it better. He also wrote down some of the stories he had made up each night. Instead of reading on the school bus and in the cafeteria, he wrote in his notebook.

The other children were used to seeing him reading all the time, so they were curious to know what he could possibly be writing about.

One day two of the children, Mark and Conrad, asked him. Peter told them about his wonderful camping trip. He showed them one of the stories he had written.

The things he had done sounded so interesting. The other boys wished they could have gone camping, too. "Have you really got a rock collection?" Conrad asked.

"Sure, I've got lots of rocks. Want to see them?"

After school, Mark and Conrad went to Peter's house, and he showed them the rocks, which he had arranged neatly in front of some books on a bookshelf.

They were impressed with the rocks, but even more impressed that Peter owned so many books. "Are all the books about rocks?" Mark said.

Peter laughed. "No. They're about all kinds of things." He showed them some of the pictures of giant spiders and unusual animals and told them what he had read about them.

Conrad liked a book about butterflies, so Peter lent it to him. He lent a book about giants to Mark.

After that, the two boys became his friends. Before long, they were all exchanging books.

Peter didn't have as much time to read as he had before, but he did have fun with Mark and Conrad. When he wasn't with them, he wrote stories. The rest of the time he was still Peter the Bookworm, but no one called him that anymore. Not even Margaret.

Draw Us a Face

Mrs. Adam was full of magic. Every night, when Margaret and Peter went to bed, she would tuck them in, kiss them good night, and then draw new faces with her finger right over their real faces.

"Now you are a big lion," she might say to Margaret. "Here are your lion eyes, your lion nose, and your lion whiskers. Now here is your lion mane." Then she would tickle Margaret all over her face to draw the mane. "Help! I don't want you to eat me up!" she would cry and rush quickly out of the room.

Then Margaret would really be a lion. She was a very big, strong lion—so big and strong that all the hunters were after her. She had to lie very still and not even swoosh her tail or move a single inch, or else they would capture her. So she would lie very quietly under the bushes until she fell asleep. But the next morning she would become Margaret again when she woke up.

Sometimes Mrs. Adam would draw a crocodile on Peter's real face. That was hard to do because crocodiles have such big mouths, so she would have to draw a big mouth that went right down to Peter's chest. "You are a very fat, lazy crocodile," she would say.

Then Peter the crocodile would lie at the water's edge in the sun, with only one eye open, patiently waiting to catch a nice juicy frog to eat. But after a while, the sun would make him so sleepy that his one opened eye would close, and he would fall fast alseep.

The next morning, though, he was Peter again.

Sometimes their magic mother would draw a bear face on Margaret. "Here are your eyes, here is your little nose, and here is your mouth," she would say. "Oh, what a sticky mouth! Have you been eating honey again, to store up for the winter?"

Mrs. Adam could also draw whole circuses on Peter's face. Sometimes he became a clown or a barking seal or a trapeze artist. Peter would fall right off his bed, thinking so hard about being a trapeze artist.

Sometimes Mrs. Adam would draw Margaret and Peter's friends' faces on them. "Now you're Laurie," she might say. "Laurie is very unhappy today." Then she would draw tears on Margaret's face.

She would draw a big frown on Peter's face. "Now you're Timothy. He's very upset because his bicycle is broken. His eyes are so BIG—just like this..." Then she would draw enormous circles around his eyes.

"Draw Caroline! Draw Damien! Draw Amy!" the children would beg, but when their mother grew tired of drawing faces, she would draw pictures of Margaret and Peter sleeping.

"These are your eyes when you're sleeping," she would say and draw two long lines over their eyes. Then she would make snoring noises. "Now you're snoring, and you're fast asleep." They would laugh and make snoring noises, too, until they really were asleep and their eyes really did look like two lines on their faces.

Oh, Mrs. Adam had all kinds of magic in her fingertips. She could draw sunglasses, beards, mustaches, and freckles on their faces.

She could draw cowboy hats, sailor hats, Indian hats, and lady hats on their heads.

She could draw flowers and feathers and fancy combs right in Margaret's hair.

She could even turn them into the Easter bunny with floppy ears... or Santa Claus with a beard... or a Halloween pumpkin with two teeth and a big grin.

She could make them look sad or glad or silly or mad... or look like each other, or look like their dad.

One night Mr. and Mrs. Adam went out. The baby-sitter didn't have the magic to draw faces. She did read them a story, but it wasn't as much fun.

Margaret didn't like to go to sleep just being herself. She twisted this way and that way, trying to sleep. She put her feet up so straight that her blanket became a tent.

That was lovely. Now Margaret became an Indian lying on the floor of her tent. Soon Margaret the Indian was fast asleep.

Peter missed having a new face, too. He crept out of bed and borrowed his father's flashlight. Then he read one of his beloved books under the covers until he fell asleep.

The next day their mother drew Indian faces on Margaret and Peter with real colored chalk, and they were Indians all afternoon. When they came in for dinner, they told their mother to close her eyes because they had a surprise for her. When she did, they each drew circles and lines on one of her cheeks. Then Peter put a feather in her hair.

When she looked in the mirror, she saw that she was an Indian, too!

When their father saw them all painted up, he laughed and laughed. "This family certainly knows how to make its own happy times!" he said.